Dear Parents,

Welcome to the Scholastic Reader series. We have taken over 80 years of experience with teachers, parents, and children and put it into a program that is designed to match your child's interests and skills.

Level 1—Short sentences and stories made up of words kids can sound out using their phonics skills and words that are important to remember.

Level 2—Longer sentences and stories with words kids need to know and new "big" words that they will want to know.

Level 3—From sentences to paragraphs to longer stories, these books have large "chunks" of texts and are made up of a rich vocabulary.

Level 4—First chapter books with more words and fewer pictures.

It is important that children learn to read well enough to succeed in school and beyond. Here are ideas for reading this book with your child:

- Look at the book together. Encourage your child to read the title and make a prediction about the story.
- Read the book together. Encourage your child to sound out words when appropriate. When your child struggles, you can help by providing the word.
- Encourage your child to retell the story. This is a great way to check for comprehension.
- Have your child take the fluency test on the last page to check progress.

Scholastic Readers are designed to support your child's efforts to learn how to read at every age and every stage. Thank you for helping your child learn to read and love to read.

— **Francie Alexander**
Chief Education Officer
Scholastic Education

To Deborah, Charles,
Danielle, and David Patton—
our friends in any weather
—A.S.M.

To my best friends Taz and Lin
—K.W.M.

Text copyright © 1999 by Angela Shelf Medearis.
Illustrations copyright © 1999 by Ken Wilson-Max.
Fluency activities copyright © 2003 Scholastic Inc.
All rights reserved. Published by Scholastic Inc.
SCHOLASTIC, CARTWHEEL BOOKS, and associated logos
are trademarks and/or registered trademarks of Scholastic Inc.

Library of Congress Cataloging-in-Publication Data is available.

ISBN: 0-439-61912-2

10 9 8 7 6 5 4 3 2 1   03   04   05   06   07
Printed in the U.S.A. 23 • First printing, February 1999

Best Friends in the Snow

by **Angela Shelf Medearis**

Illustrated by **Ken Wilson-Max**

Scholastic Reader — Level 1

SCHOLASTIC INC.

Cartwheel ·B·O·O·K·S·®

New York Toronto London Auckland Sydney
Mexico City New Delhi Hong Kong Buenos Aires

It's cold outside,
but we are warm,
with hats and coats
and mittens on.

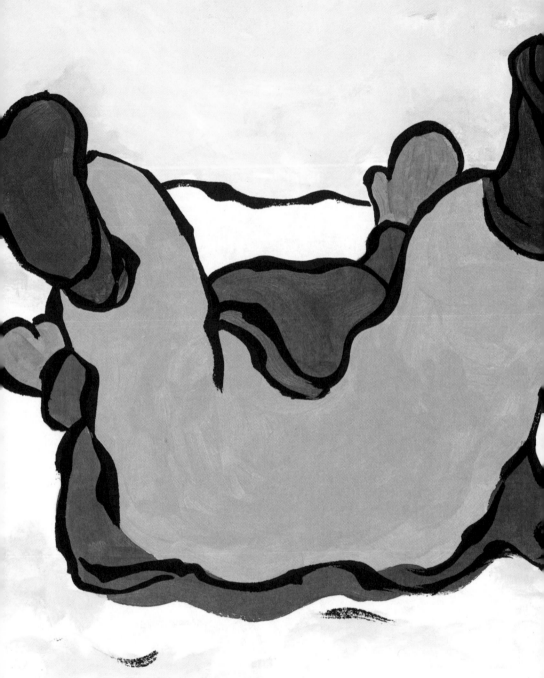

We fall once.
We fall twice.

We fall again
on the frozen ice.

We slip and slide
down a hill.

We make a snowman.
Let's call him Bill.

We catch snowflakes
in the air.

We make snow angels
here and there.

We build a fort.

We squeeze in tight.

We're ready for
a snowball fight.

We like
to play
in the snow
together.

Best friends are fun
in snowy weather.

All Mixed Up

These sentences are all mixed up.
Can you unscramble them?

tight We in squeeze

a build fort We

call Bill Let's him

Word Find Fun

Do you see **hat**, **coat**, **scarf**, and **mittens** in the Word Find? Look across and down.

B O S C A R F

T R H O P R A

S H A A R G L

M I T T E N S

Dot to Dot

Connect the dots from A to Z and you'll see a snowy surprise!

Words in Rhyme

The word **sun** rhymes with the word **fun**.
Can you find words in the story that
rhyme with these words?

rest

freeze

glide

kittens

bats

tall

flip

At the Beginning

In each row, point to the word that begins with the same letter as the first word in the row.

cold   slip   lots   coats

frosty   frozen   throw   ice

snow   slide   friends   hill

play   fun   weather   pals

mittens   warm   slide   make

Story Time

The friends in the story have fun together on a snowy day.
Tell a story about a fun time you had with your friends on a snowy day.

ANSWERS

All Mixed Up

We squeeze in tight.

We build a fort.

Let's call him Bill.

_____

Word Find Fun

B O S C A R F

T R H O P R A

S H A A R G L

M I T T E N S

_____

Dot to Dot

Words in Rhyme

rest/best

freeze/squeeze

glide/slide, outside

kittens/mittens

bats/hats

tall/fall

flip/slip

_____

At the Beginning

coats

frozen

slide

pals

make

_____

Story Time

Answers will vary.